WIThDRAWN

Millie Loves Ants

To Jack and Tom, with love. May you find ants too, and Millie.
And to Sue and her magic, and her girls, with love and memories
of mooching in the valley — Jackie French

For Sophie x — Sue deGennaro

Angus&Robertson

An imprint of HarperCollins*Children'sBooks*, Australia

First published in Australia in 2017
Paperback edition published in 2018
by HarperCollins*Publishers* Australia Pty Limited
ABN 36 009 913 517
harpercollins.com.au

HarperCollins*Publishers*
Level 13, 201 Elizabeth Street, Sydney NSW 2000, Australia
Unit D1, 63 Apollo Drive, Rosedale, Auckland 0632, New Zealand
A 53, Sector 57, Noida, UP, India
1 London Bridge Street, London SE1 9GF, United Kingdom
2 Bloor Street East, 20th floor, Toronto, Ontario M4W 1A8, Canada
195 Broadway, New York NY 10007, USA

National Library of Australia Cataloguing-in-Publication entry:

French, Jackie, author.
    Millie loves ants / Jackie French ; Sue deGennaro.
    9781460751787 (hardback)
    9781460751794 (paperback)
    For pre-school age.
    Ants—Juvenile fiction.
    Ants—Behaviour—Juvenile fiction.
    deGennaro, Sue, illustrator.
A823.3

Cover and internal design by Stephanie Spartels, Studio Spartels
The illustrations in this book were created in watercolour, pencil and gouache
Colour reproduction by Graphic Print Group, Adelaide
Printed and bound in China by RR Donnelley on 140gsm Woodfree

5 4 3 2   19 20

Jackie French & Sue deGennaro

Millie Loves Ants

Angus&Robertson
An imprint of HarperCollins*Children'sBooks*

My friend Millie
just loves ants.

Her whole world
is ants,
ants,
ants.

10/19 BF

Ants in pot plants
on our path.

Ants that live beneath our bath.

Ants that crawl up in my pants.

Ants that make me jump and dance!

Ants in the kitchen,

ants in the shed.

Ants on a picnic,

ants on my bed.

Ants that live in hollow trees.

Ants that make their homes of leaves.

Ants in tunnels,
ants in mounds,

drag
down debris
to their towns.

Small but mighty hunter ants

help make soil to feed the plants.

Queen ants fly before the rain.

If there's just a chance
of ants,

Millie's nose must do
its dance.

Why so **many**, spiny friend?

Millie trundles through the trees, wildflowers bending in the breeze.

Where the
sunlit
tussocks
glow,

and dusty wombats
dig below.

where most of Millie's
ants will go!

And I follow
– now I know